Happy Christmas, Lulu

To Sue, Nigel and Lucy
with love

ORCHARD BOOKS

338 Euston Road, London NW1 3BH

Orchard Books Australia

Level 17/207 Kent Street, Sydney, NSW 2000

First published in 2002 by Orchard Books
First published in paperback in 2003
This edition published in 2009
ISBN 978 1 40830 343 6
Text and illustrations © Caroline Uff 2002

10 9 8 7 6 5 4 3 2 1

Printed in China

Orchard Books is a division of Hachette Children's Books, an Hachette Livre UK company.
www.hachettelivre.co.uk

Happy Christmas, Lulu

Caroline Uff

ORCHARD BOOKS

Hello
Lulu.

Are you
getting ready
for Christmas?

Glue, glue, stick, stick.

What a lovely glittery card. "For my Granny," says Lulu.

Time to get the Christmas tree.

It's cold outside.
Wrap up warm,
Lulu.

Brr! Brr!

"Look at our beautiful tree," says Lulu.

Twinkle, twinkle, fairy lights.

Lulu loves her big sister's Christmas play.

"Away in a manger..." sings Lulu with all the other children.

What a lot of
shopping bags, Lulu.

Oops! Don't drop them.

Lulu and her big sister are busy cooking.

Mmm! Those biscuits look delicious.

Hooray,
it's Christmas day!

What a lot of presents.
And one for Lulu's
puppy too.

Woof!
Woof!

Lulu loves
her presents.

Lulu's baby brother loves playing with the paper. Scrunch! Scrunch!

Yum! Yum! Christmas dinner for everyone.

Happy Christmas Lulu!